To <u>You</u>
All the readers and friends of Abby!!

Chapter 1

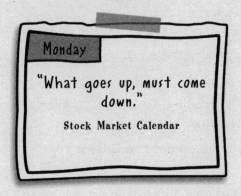

Monday

"What goes up, must come down."

Stock Market Calendar

Nooooooooooo!
Every night I've been studying math facts for half an hour. Last week I got my first A on a math quiz!!!! Ms. Kantor told me if I keep it up, I might get a B+ on my next report card. Wow! Hooray!

My math grade is going up. MUST it come down???? _NO! NO! NO!_

This quote is true for:
-balloons
-airplanes

—birds
—eyebrows

This quote is not true for:
—Abby's math grade
—Abby's ability to add, subtract, multiply, and divide
—Abby's happiness quotient

Don't believe everything you read in calendars. Even if you have the world's biggest collection. Even if calendars cover the walls of your room and are stacked in piles in your closet.

"I have candy bars in my backpack," Jessica said. She unzipped the pack and took out a plastic bag. "Want one?"

"No eating in my room," Abby said. "We can go downstairs."

Jessica looked at her best friend in surprise. "You never used to mind."

"That was before I painted my room purple," Abby explained, gesturing toward the shiny purple walls and furniture in her room.

Abby had coated everything in the room with her favorite color: walls, desk, bureau, chair, and lamp. Her sister Eva had sewed purple polka-dotted curtains for the windows, and her sister Isabel had donated a purple spread for the bed. Now her room was a Palace of Purple.

Everything was purple except for the floor!

"Okay," Jessica said. She swung the bag of chocolate bars back and forth. "Let's go. It's left over from Halloween."

"Yum," Abby said.

The two girls went downstairs.

On the landing, Abby stopped to pet T-Jeff. The kitten rubbed his face against her leg and purred.

"I wish I could pet him," Jessica said longingly. "I'm so allergic to cats."

"So is Alex," Abby said, referring to her younger brother. "Isabel and I have to take turns vacuuming the living room every day."

Isabel and Abby shared ownership of T-Jeff. He was originally Abby's kitten, but she hadn't been able to take care of him by herself. Her older sister had taken over most of the work. She had also insisted on naming the kitten Thomas Jefferson. Abby had shortened it to T-Jeff.

"His name sounds like a new kind of dinosaur," Jessica commented.

"Tyrannosaurus Jefferson," Abby joked. "The kitten that strikes fear into the hearts of dust balls, mice, strings, and yarn."

They crossed the living room where Abby's brother, Alex, was watching a show on TV. In the dining room, schoolbooks were stacked on the table. The smell of cooking came from the kitchen.

"Hi, Jessica. Good to see you." Abby's father, Paul Hayes, was standing at the stove, stirring a pot of chili. "Can you stay for dinner tonight?"

Jessica shook her head. "No thanks, I can't. My mom and I are getting Chinese food tonight."

"Any special occasion?" Paul Hayes asked.

Jessica nodded. She took out two chocolate bars and gave one to Abby. She unwrapped her own and took a bite from it.

"Yes, it's a special occasion," she said after a moment. She took a breath. "It's sort of a celebration. I'm going to visit my father."

"You are?" Abby cried. "When????"

Jessica hadn't seen her father for a long time, although he called and wrote her regularly.

"Soon," Jessica said. "As soon as he enrolls me in

school. Maybe by next week. That's the end of the cycle."

Abby stared at her best friend. She couldn't utter a word. "You're going to school there?" she finally said.

"It's only for one marking period," Jessica said. "Three months. I'll be back in the spring."

Paul Hayes lowered the gas under the chili pot and put down the wooden spoon. "When did this happen, Jessica?" he asked gently.

"Last week," Jessica said. "My dad called my mother and offered to send a plane ticket. He just got married. He wants me to get to know his new family."

"He got married?" Abby cried. "Why didn't you tell me!"

"I don't know." Jessica shrugged and looked away. "His new wife has two daughters," she finally said.

"You have stepsisters?" Abby said in disbelief. "And you didn't say anything?"

Jessica was an only child. She had always been envious of Abby's brother and twin sisters. She had always wanted siblings of her own.

"They're ten and seven — just like you and Alex," Jessica said, as if that explained her silence.

"When did you last see your dad?" Paul Hayes asked.

Jessica broke off another piece of her candy bar. "Four years ago. Before he moved to Oregon."

"That's a long trip," Paul Hayes commented. "But four years is a long time not to see your father."

"Yes," Abby agreed. Was that why Jessica hadn't said anything to her? She couldn't imagine not seeing her father for four years. She'd miss him if he left for four days!

"I've never been on a plane before," Jessica confessed.

"Are you flying by yourself?" Abby asked. She glanced at her father. She had asked her parents to let her fly unaccompanied to Grandma Emma's house. They had always said no.

Jessica shook her head. "Someone's going to meet me when I change planes in Chicago."

The three of them were quiet for a moment.

"A plane trip to Oregon, a different school, a visit with your father, a stepmother, and two new siblings — anything else?" Paul Hayes asked. "Any more changes planned?"

"No." Jessica smiled.

"That's enough!" Abby cried.

There was a silence.

"What are your stepsisters' names?" Abby asked.

"Danielle and Dakota." Jessica searched in the pocket of her overalls. "I guess I forgot the picture. Danielle is our age. I'll be in class with her. She sounds pretty nice."

"At least she's not named after a state, like her sister," Abby said. "What if your parents named you Rhode Island? Or Vermont? Or Illinois? Or *Massachusetts*?"

"Massachusetts Hayes. That has a ring to it," Abby's father said. "I wish your mother and I had thought of it when you were born."

"Dad!" Abby protested.

"She gets her sense of humor from me," Paul Hayes said to Jessica. He took the salad spinner from the cupboard. "Abby, will you get the lettuce out of the refrigerator?"

Abby searched in the vegetable bin. "Can we put olives and carrots in the salad?" she asked.

"Of course." Her father nodded. "Your mother is going to miss you," he said to Jessica.

"She's taking a trip to Greece," Jessica said.

"Wonderful!" Paul Hayes said. "I wonder if we have any relatives who will take Isabel, Eva, Abby, and Alex for a month or two?"

"Dad!" Abby cried.

"It won't be easy." Her father winked at the two girls. "No sane person would take all of you for more than an hour!"

Abby glanced at Jessica to see how she was taking her father's humor. Jessica was smiling.

"I hope my dad is as nice as yours," she said as she and Abby headed back to Abby's room.

"It's funny — " Abby began, then stopped.

"What?" Jessica asked.

Abby shrugged. "Nothing." She had almost said it was funny that Jessica didn't know whether her dad was nice or not.

It wasn't really funny at all.

"I can't wait to meet Danielle and Dakota!" Jessica blurted out. "It's like having two instant sisters!"

"Add water and mix," Abby joked.

"One minute they're not there and then, pouf! They're here!" Jessica said. "It's like magic."

Abby nodded. "Now *you're* here, but in a week you won't be," she said. She still couldn't get used to the idea. And why hadn't Jessica said anything to her?

Jessica plunked herself down on Abby's bed. "What do you think it'll be like, Abby? Having sisters, I mean."

"Noisy," Abby said. She had a lot of experience with sisters.

"Don't you think it'll be wonderful?" Jessica sighed.

Abby made a face. "You can have the Twin Terrors anytime."

"I want sisters of my own," Jessica insisted.

Abby walked over to her desk and flipped open a calendar. "Aren't friends good enough?" she asked.

"You don't understand," Jessica said.

The two girls looked at each other. Abby caught her breath. There was so much more she wanted to say, but somehow she couldn't say a word.

Chapter 2

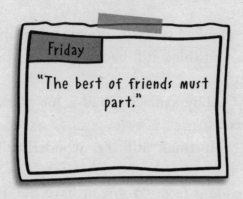

Friday

"The best of friends must part."

What my sister Isabel said after I hung up the phone with Jessica.

Why do the best of friends have to part???? I don't want to part from Jessica for three whole months!

She called while we were eating breakfast this morning to tell me that she's leaving on Sunday. That's only two days from now! That's five days earlier than she thought. She has to leave right away. That's <u>no fair</u>!

I'm not ready for Jessica to go so soon!

<u>How Many Ways Will I Miss</u>
<u>My Best Friend?</u>

1. No one to cheer me up when my SuperSibs argue and fight.

2. No one to talk to when everyone in my family is busy.

3. No one to explain the math problems I don't understand!

4. No one to laugh with when Brianna brags too much.

5. No one to have sleepovers with on weekends.

6. No one to —

<u>Enough!!!!</u> I can't think about any more ways I'll miss Jessica or I'll start crying right now.

My mother said three months isn't long. Before I know it, Jessica will be home again.

My mother is wrong! Three months is <u>for-ever</u>!!!!!!

Jessica called an emergency All-Friends meeting for lunch today. She, Natalie,

Sarah, and I will all sit together at the same lunch table.

I am so sad!

Will I be able to eat even a bite?

Notes to self:

1. Pack lunch I don't like. (I won't miss it if I'm too upset to eat.)

2. Bring container of sliced onions. (No one will wonder why I'm crying.)

3. Put tissues in lunch box instead of napkins.

4. Wear sunglasses to hide red eyes.

Today is the last day I will spend with Jessica for three months! Tomorrow she has to pack her suitcase and shop with her mother for holiday gifts.

On Sunday, she leaves.

My father said he'd take me to the airport to say good-bye. (Thanks, Dad!) At least I'll be able to put it off until the very last minute.

"I can't believe you're going so soon!" Natalie wailed. "You'll miss the winter holidays and everything!"

"I'm not exactly missing them," Jessica pointed out. "I'll celebrate them with my father and his new family."

"But you won't be *here*," Abby said.

"No," Jessica agreed. She unwrapped a straw and poked it into her milk carton. "But I'll be *there*."

Sarah ran her fingers through her short, curly hair. "We won't be able to go skiing together during vacation."

"Or sledding," Abby said.

"Or show each other our presents," Natalie added.

The four fifth-grade girls sat at one end of the cafeteria table. Abby, Natalie, and Jessica were all in Ms. Kantor's class and had been good friends for a while. Sarah was in Mrs. McMillan's class. She and Jessica had recently become friends while working on a science fair project.

Natalie unwrapped a turkey sandwich, then put it down untouched. "I hate saying good-bye!"

"Me, too," Abby said. She wasn't *really* saying

good-bye now, since her dad was taking her to the airport. But she couldn't tell that to Natalie and Sarah. What if they wanted to come, too?

Abby wanted to be the last person to see Jessica. She was *her* best friend.

Jessica sighed. "I'm happy and I'm sad." She pushed away her milk carton. "I wish I could be in two places at once."

"What did Ms. Kantor say when you told her?" Sarah asked.

"She said she hoped I had a great visit with my dad," Jessica said, "and not to worry about missing anything."

"Gee, I wish she'd say that to me!" Natalie said.

"I wish she'd say that to me about math!" Abby said. "Even though I'm getting better at it."

"Do you think your new teacher will be as nice as Ms. Kantor?" Sarah asked Jessica.

"Danielle said she was," Jessica confided. "Her name is Ms. Allen. Danielle said Ms. Allen loves science."

"Just like you!" Sarah exclaimed.

"Will you have creative writing, too?" Natalie asked. "I bet you won't get a teacher like Ms. Bunder!"

"I don't know," Jessica said. "I hope there's a good art teacher, too."

Abby said nothing. She didn't want to think about Jessica in another classroom with new teachers and friends. She didn't want to think about her drawing funny pictures that Abby wouldn't see or helping someone else with her math problems. And who would Abby read her creative writing assignments to if Jessica wasn't there?

"Are you nervous about seeing your father again?" Natalie asked.

"We've talked on the phone a lot," Jessica said with a shrug. "And he's sent cards and presents. It's not like I don't know him."

Sarah nodded. "I bet you'll have a great time."

Jessica picked at a loose thread on her overalls. "There's just one thing I'm worried about," she began. "Not school, not home, not friends — "

"What else is there?" Abby interrupted.

"Work!" Jessica said. "I have dog-walking and baby-sitting jobs. I can't do them when I'm in Oregon."

"Unless you have a secret double," Abby said.

Sarah leaned forward. "*We* can help you!"

Abby wished that *she* had said it first. Then Jessica would be smiling at her instead of Sarah.

"Yes," Abby echoed. "I'll take over one of your jobs."

"Me, too," Natalie said.

"Really?" Jessica said. "Are you sure you want to?"

The four girls looked at each other.

"Why not?" Natalie said. "We'll earn money, won't we?"

Jessica nodded. "I have four dogs to walk every day after school. And baby-sitting three times a week. I earn twenty dollars a week for dog walking and eighteen to twenty-five dollars a week for baby-sitting."

"I'll dog walk!" Natalie and Sarah said at the same time.

"You can divide it up," Jessica suggested. "Each of you take two dogs. I'll set it up."

"I'll baby-sit," Abby offered. She was secretly relieved that Natalie and Sarah wanted to take over the dog walking. She had tried it before. Leashes got tangled; dogs chased anything that moved; and there were nasty messes to clean up.

Baby-sitting was much easier and much more fun.

"You'll be a mother's helper," Jessica explained. "Do you remember Geoffrey?"

Abby frowned. "The one who put maple syrup in your hair?"

"He's a lot better now," Jessica said quickly. "I've got him trained. I'll tell you everything before I go. Once you know the secret, it's easy."

"Good," Abby said.

"Don't worry," Natalie said to Jessica. "We'll take care of everything."

Jessica threw her arms around her friends. "You're all the greatest! I'll call Geoffrey's mom and the dog owners tonight and let them know."

As the girls walked slowly out of the cafeteria, Ms. Kantor hurried past them.

"The meeting starts in three minutes," she reminded them. "Hurry upstairs to the library!"

"We almost missed it!" Abby exclaimed. "All we've been thinking about is Jessica leaving!"

Ms. Kantor nodded. "I know you want to say good-bye, but we're counting on you! Don't forget that."

"Movie night?" Sarah asked.

"Yes," Natalie said.

A few days ago, the class had read about floods in another part of the country. They were planning a movie and popcorn night in the school gymnasium to raise money for families who had lost their homes. All the profits would be donated to a disaster relief fund.

"I'm doing publicity," Abby said. "I'm going to make posters and put them up in stores and schools."

"I'm on the cleanup committee," Jessica said. She made a face. "Or *was*. I won't be able to wash tables and throw away garbage if I'm in Oregon."

"You're going to miss all the fun!" Natalie joked.

"Are you on the cleanup committee, too?" Sarah asked.

"I'm on the committee that chooses the movie," Natalie replied. "We're also in charge of movie and equipment rental."

"Pick a sports film!" Sarah urged. "Or something with animals."

"I'm going to vote for a fantasy movie," Natalie said. "That's *my* favorite."

"What about a comedy?" Abby asked. "They're always popular."

"So are sad movies," Jessica pointed out.

The girls headed toward the library.

"Whatever happens, you have to let me know,"

Jessica said. "You're all going to e-mail me, aren't you?"

"Of course!" Abby promised.

"Sure," Sarah said.

"Yes," Natalie said.

Ms. Kantor waved the girls into the library. "Hurry up!" she called. "We're waiting for you!"

Sarah said good-bye and headed back downstairs. Abby, Jessica, and Natalie ran into the library.

Chapter 3

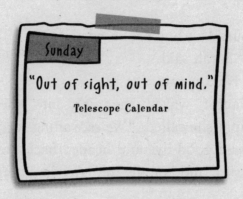

Sunday

"Out of sight, out of mind."

Telescope Calendar

Today Jessica gets on a plane. She is going to Oregon. She'll be out of sight, but she <u>won't</u> be out of mind.

I'll think about her all the time. I'll e-mail her every day.

I'll write her about movie night. I'll tell her my math quiz scores. I'll write about Geoffrey. (I hope there's not too much to tell!)

<u>Almost New Year's Resolutions</u>

1. Become a great baby-sitter.

2. Let Jessica know that her job is in good hands.

3. Make sure that she can come back and find everything the way it was.

4. Remind Jessica every day how much I miss her!!!

At the meeting on Friday, we tried to think of a name for our movie night fund-raiser. Ms. Kantor kept asking me if I had any ideas. I didn't. She asked what was on my mind. I couldn't tell her. (Hint: It wasn't movie night.)

Fortunately, my classmates had lots of ideas.

<u>Ms. Kantor's Fifth-Graders' Marvelous Movie Night Names</u>

1. An Evening of Movies and Popcorn
2. Fabulous Food and Film Festival
3. The Silver Screen Savers
4. Munch and Watch
5. Lancaster Film Fair

And the winner is . . . The Silver Screen Savers. Do you think that's a catchy name for the evening? I do! Here's what I'm going to write on the poster:

THE SILVER SCREEN SAVERS

present a night of Family Fun, Entertainment, and Refreshments.
Relax, Watch a Movie, and Enjoy Delicious Refreshments!

Movie: TBA (To Be Announced)
Date: Friday night
Time: 7:00 P.M.
Place: Lancaster Elementary Cafeteria and Gymnasium
Admission: $3.00 per person

All profits will be donated to charity!

 I'm going to write the names of the refreshments up and down the sides of the poster. Popcorn! Brownies! Cider!

Muffins! There will be pictures, too.

I hope we offer popcorn, brownies, and cider. Brianna is on the refreshment committee, and she has other ideas.

Refreshments Brianna Wants to Serve

Petit fours (huh?), cheesecake cookies (really?), and glazed chocolate almond crescents (huh? again)

Mulled cider, sparkling grape juice, mango punch

Refreshments the Other Kids on the Committee Want to Serve

Popcorn, brownies, vanilla cupcakes, and donuts (hooray!)

Cider, hot chocolate, and orange juice

Number of Other Kids on the Committee

Four

Number of Briannas on the Committee

One

Reason We Might All Eat Petits Fours on Movie Night Instead of Donuts

No one wants to argue with Brianna!

Question: What is a petit four? And why <u>does</u> Brianna want us to eat them instead of brownies?

When we decide on refreshments and the movie, I'm going to print out a poster, make hundreds of copies, and put them up in supermarkets, restaurants, bookstores, and schools. I will call the local radio and TV stations and ask them to make announcements. Hundreds of people will show up for the Silver Screen Savers movie night. Ms. Kantor's class will make buckets of money for the families who lost their homes!

What color paper shall I print out the posters on? Electric blue? Lime green? Bright yellow? Vivid orange? Wild purple? One of them or all of them?
What font will I use?
What does a petit four look like?

Should I sign each poster "An Abby Hayes Original!"?

INTERRUPTION!!!
Dad just told me to get ready. It's time to go to the airport. I've been trying not to think about it.

BOOHOO!!!!

"Parting is such sweet sorrow."
William Shakespeare said that. So did Isabel this morning at breakfast.
Why is parting "sweet"? I don't think so! It is painful, agonizing, sad, desperate, unhappy, and miserable. There is nothing sweet about it!

Dad just knocked on my door. I have to go.

A Heartrending Tale of Incredible Tragedy
by Abby Hayes

It was a dark and stormy night.

No, it wasn't.

Actually, it was a sunny and pleasant morning. But it should have been a dark and stormy night.

Paul Hayes and Abby Hayes got into the minivan. Paul Hayes put the key in the ignition.

"Wait a minute," he said to his daughter. "I forgot my coffee."

"Dad!" Abby cried. "I don't want to miss saying good-bye to Jessica!"

"Don't worry," Paul Hayes said. He ran back into the house. A minute later, he came back with a thermos filled with coffee. He was whistling.

"Remind me to buy bagels on the way home," he said as they pulled out of the driveway.

"Bagels?"

"Onion, sesame, and cinnamon raisin," her father said. "And a tub of cream cheese, too."

Abby sighed. This was one of the saddest moments of her life, and her father was talking about breakfast.

At the airport, Abby and her father

walked to the gate to find Jessica and her mother. As they approached the waiting area, Abby suddenly wanted to turn around and run. Maybe if she didn't say good-bye, Jessica wouldn't leave.

Her father touched her arm. "You okay?"

Abby nodded.

Jessica was looking out the window at the tarmac. She was wearing overalls, a striped sweater, and sneakers, and she carried a backpack and a book. She was watching baggage handlers load suitcases onto the plane. She looked happier than Abby expected.

Her mother stood next to her, with a worried frown on her face.

"You know what happens when you get to Chicago?" her mother asked.

"Yes, Mom," Jessica began. She turned around suddenly.

"Abby! You're here!" she cried.

Abby tried to smile. She couldn't say anything.

Jessica's mother greeted Abby and her father. "Thanks for coming," she said. "We're happy you came to see Jessica off."

"I brought this for you." Abby thrust a paper bag into Jessica's hand.

Jessica's eyes lit up. "Can I open it now?"

"Sure. Why not?"

"Don't leave us in suspense, Jessica," Paul Hayes said.

Jessica pulled out a giant chocolate bar with almonds. It was her favorite kind.

"It's for the plane," Abby said. "In case you get hungry."

The next present was a bright turquoise journal with a package of gel pens taped to its cover.

"Just what you need," Jessica's mother commented. "Now you can write down everything that happens to you."

"Thanks!" Jessica said. "I love it!"

"There's more," Abby said.

"More?" Jessica repeated. She pulled out a calendar. On the cover was a photo of Abby and Jessica on Rollerblades. The name of the calendar was printed in large purple letters: OREGON ADVENTURES.

"I made it on the computer," Abby explained. "It's a three-month calendar for your visit. Look inside."

Jessica flipped through the calendar. Each page had pictures of Abby and Jessica, from kindergarten through fifth grade. The days of the week were decorated with soccer balls, rainbows, and butterflies.

"You even put quotes for every month!" Jessica cried. "This is the greatest!"

"And that's not all," Paul Hayes said, handing her a small package with a blue bow. "This is from the rest of the Hayes family."

"A disposable camera!" Jessica exclaimed.

"We hope you have a fine visit with your father and his family," Paul Hayes said, "and bring us back a snapshot or two."

"Don't take pictures of people's ankles, like Alex does," Abby warned her.

Jessica hugged Abby. "You're the best friend in the world!"

"I hope you like Danielle and Dakota," Abby said. "But not better than any of the friends you have here!"

"Our flight is now boarding," a crew member announced. "Those sitting in rows thirty-six to twenty-four, those requiring assistance, and families with young children may now begin to board."

Jessica examined her ticket. "I'm in row eleven," she said. "I don't board yet." She put the presents into her backpack.

"Remember, the airline will send an escort to meet you in Chicago," her mother began.

Jessica clapped her hand to her forehead. "I forgot!"

Her mother frowned. "The escort? Jessica, you can't forget!"

"Not that." Jessica turned to Abby. "I forgot to tell you the secret."

"Rows twenty-four to twelve may now board," the announcer intoned.

"The secret?" Abby asked.

It sounded like a mystery novel. Did Jessica know where treasure was buried?

What problems were going to be on the next math test? Whom Brianna had a crush on?

"Of how to handle Geoffrey," Jessica explained.

"Geoffrey!" Abby exclaimed. "Oh, no!" Jessica had told her all about his pranks and mischief. She didn't want to show up without a plan. It was her key to success.

"Don't worry," Jessica said. "I know how to deal with Geoffrey. You have to –"

"All remaining passengers may now board the plane."

"What's the secret?" Abby cried.

"I'll e-mail you!" Jessica promised. She kissed her mother good-bye and handed the flight attendant her ticket.

"Don't forget!" Abby called. "I'm watching him on Tuesday!"

Jessica waved one last time and disappeared down the ramp.

Chapter 4

Tuesday

"No man's knowledge here can go beyond his experience."
—John Locke

1001 Things to Do with String Calendar

Whoever wrote that quote never had a best friend. (Or does the quote only apply to "man" and not "girl"?)

My knowledge of Geoffrey <u>does</u> go beyond my experience.

That's because Jessica e-mailed me her top secret tips on how to deal with him.

<u>Jessica's Best Geoffrey-Taming Tips</u>

1. When he starts having tantrums, read him <u>Itty Baby in the Bath</u>.

2. If he says no to every-thing, get out his dump truck.

3. When all else fails, give him chocolate pudding.

It's easy! Anyone can do it! Thanks to Jessica's experience, I have all the knowledge I need.

I will keep her job ready for her.

When she comes home, it'll be as if she never left.

She'll be _so_ grateful and happy!

Our friendship will be good, better, best, bester!!! (Is "bester" a word? It should be!)

"Wish me luck," Abby said as she and Natalie walked home from school together. "I'm going to Geoffrey's house for my first day of baby-sitting."

Natalie raised her eyebrows. "You need more than luck with Geoffrey. I watched him once. He's a terror."

"Jessica said you just have to know how to handle him."

"Really?" Natalie didn't sound convinced. "I'm glad _I'm_ dog walking." She glanced at her watch. "Half an hour until I start. I can't wait!"

"I have all of Jessica's baby-sitting tips right here.

With her advice, I can't fail," Abby insisted, pulling a crumpled sheet of paper from her pocket. "See?"

Natalie glanced briefly at the paper and shrugged. "How's Jessica?" she asked.

"She has to share a room with Danielle. She said the room is really messy."

"I bet Jessica hates that!"

All her friends knew that Jessica was a neat freak. Clothes were always folded or hung in the closet. Papers were organized in folders. The bed was always made.

"And Danielle likes to dress up and go to parties," Abby said. "She has millions of friends."

"She sounds like Jessica's opposite," Natalie commented.

"I hope Danielle isn't like Brianna," Abby said.

Natalie made a face. "Did you hear her today?" She flipped an imaginary mane of hair over her shoulder in imitation of Brianna.

"Brownies and donuts are boring!" she proclaimed in a Brianna-like voice. "*My* committee will serve only the best and most original pastries."

"My brownies are all Broadway stars," Abby mimicked. "My donuts speak French."

"And my cider wears the coolest clothes," Natalie finished.

The two girls began to laugh.

"Good thing Victoria isn't on the refreshment committee, too," Abby said, referring to Brianna's best friend. "Or on the movie committee!"

Natalie shuddered. "She'd make us watch Tiffany Crystal videos!"

"*Ugh!*" Abby cried.

"We're arguing about the movies anyway," Natalie said. "Most of the kids on my committee want to see *Twenty-two Rottweilers.*"

"That movie about the family who adopted all the dogs?" Abby asked. "Everyone's seen it a million times!"

"I know!" Natalie said. "The other movie everyone wants is *The Princess Mermaid.*"

"I *hate* that movie!" Abby said.

"No one can agree on a fantasy movie," Natalie said glumly. "Most of them aren't that good. The books are usually better."

"Ms. Bunder says magic takes place in your mind," Abby said. Ms. Bunder was the creative writing teacher. Creative writing was Abby's favorite subject.

"I wish the magic took place on-screen," Natalie said. "Where is the movie that *everyone* wants to see? We have to find it!"

"Yeah," Abby agreed. "Until you decide, I can't make the posters. If I don't put the posters up, no one will know about the event."

Natalie stopped. "There's Geoffrey's house."

The two-story house was painted pale blue with white trim. Neatly pruned bushes lined the yard. There was a tricycle overturned on the sidewalk.

"It's like every other house on the block," Abby said.

"But it has Geoffrey inside," Natalie warned her. "I'd rather walk a hundred dogs together than baby-sit one of him."

"He can't be that bad," Abby said. She patted her pocket. "Besides, I've got all of Jessica's secrets right here."

Natalie looked doubtful. "Well . . . good luck!" she finally said, checking her watch. "It's time for me to walk the dogs! *Hooray!!!*"

She said good-bye and hurried down the block.

Abby pulled out Jessica's e-mail and studied it one last time.

"Don't get scared by his temper tantrums," Jessica

had written. "Remain calm, find his favorite book, and start reading it."

"Okay, I will," Abby said.

Jessica's tips would make all the difference in taking care of Geoffrey. And Abby would make sure that she took care of Jessica's job.

She took a deep breath, went up the stairs, and rang the doorbell.

"You must be Abby. I'm Elaine, Geoffrey's mom." The woman who opened the door was wearing blue jeans and a sweater. She had a friendly smile. "Come in. Geoffrey is so excited that you'll be playing with him."

"Hi," Abby said. "Nice to meet you." She stepped into the hallway. There were clothes and toys scattered on the floor.

"Excuse the mess," Elaine said, running her hands through her hair.

She led Abby into a living room even messier than the hallway. "Geoffrey!" she called. "Abby's here!"

There was no answer.

"Geoffrey?!"

"BOO!" Geoffrey yelled, jumping out from behind the couch.

He was small and blond. There was a large smear of jam on his face.

"Hi, Geoffrey," Abby said. She smiled at him. "I'm Abby."

Geoffrey stared at her. He twisted his face into a terrible grimace. Then he ran to his mother and flung his arms around her legs.

"Abby is Jessica's friend," Elaine said. "She's going to play with you today."

"No!" Geoffrey said.

"Mommy has to work. Don't you want to show Abby all your toys?"

"No!" Geoffrey said.

Abby got down on her knees and picked up a fire truck. "Vroom! Vroom! Vroom!"

"You can show Abby where everything is," Elaine said. "She'll give you your favorite snack."

"Chocolate pudding," Abby said.

From behind his mother's legs, Geoffrey watched her. "I want to play with my walkie-talkie."

"Okay," Abby said. "Where is it?"

He scampered into the next room.

Elaine smiled at her. "You're going to do fine. My office is upstairs, over the garage. If you need me, come get me."

She disappeared out the back door. Geoffrey ran into the room with two walkie-talkies in his hand.

"Where's Mommy?" he demanded. "Where'd she go?"

"She's working," Abby said.

"Mommy! I want Mommy! I want her now!" Geoffrey's voice rose in pitch.

 Abby pointed to the walkie-talkies. "Don't you want to play with them?"

"Mommy! Mommy!" Geoffrey yelled.

Abby's heart raced. How had Jessica done it? She didn't have a clue what to do next.

"You can be a policeman," she said. "Or do you want to be a pilot?"

Suddenly Geoffrey stopped yelling. He handed her a walkie-talkie.

Abby breathed a sigh of relief.

"You stay here," he ordered. "I'll hide. Then I'll call you."

"Okay," Abby agreed. She sat down on the couch and waited.

Chapter 5

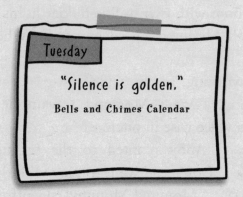

Tuesday

"Silence is golden."

Bells and Chimes Calendar

Silence is also scary, ominous, unpleasant, disturbing, upsetting, frightening, and alarming.

Especially when you're baby-sitting Geoffrey.

Especially when you don't know where he is.

Especially when you don't know where to look.

Especially when the silence goes on and on and on and on. . . .

Where is he???

One after another, Abby pushed the buttons on the walkie-talkie. "Geoffrey?" she said. "*Geoffrey?*"

There was no answer.

Abby unfolded her copy of Jessica's e-mail and scanned it quickly. Jessica had not sent her any tips on what to do if Geoffrey disappeared.

What would Jessica do in her place? Jessica always knew exactly what to do. So why didn't Abby?

"Geoffrey!!" Abby called. "Geoffrey!!!"

Abby ran from room to room, calling his name.

No Geoffrey in sight.

He wasn't in the kitchen, the dining room, or the downstairs bathroom.

Frantically she dashed upstairs. She flung open doors, peered under beds, and checked closets and shower stalls.

She ran back downstairs. Her heart was racing. What if he had gone outside? What if he had gone to a neighbor's house? What if he was already someplace she couldn't find him?

If she couldn't find Geoffrey, she'd have to find Elaine. Elaine would fire her. Abby would have to write to Jessica and admit that she'd failed to keep her job. She would have let her best friend down when Jessica needed her most.

"BOO!" Geoffrey jumped out from behind the door and made a horrible face at Abby.

Abby collapsed on the couch.

"I want chocolate pudding! Now!"

"Wait." Abby held up her hand. She had to catch her breath. She felt like she had just done the hundred-yard dash.

"Were you hiding behind the door all the time?"

Geoffrey nodded.

"Did you hear me calling you?"

He nodded again.

"Why didn't you answer?"

Geoffrey made another horrible face.

"Is that all you have to say?"

"Blub."

Abby stood up. "It's time for chocolate pudding," she said.

She marched into the kitchen, keeping a close eye on Geoffrey. She didn't think he'd hide again if chocolate pudding was in sight, but she didn't trust him for a second.

*   *   *

"Thanks again," Elaine said. She handed Abby a five- and a one-dollar bill. "You did a good job."

"Uh, thanks." Abby glanced at Geoffrey. He was hanging on to his mother's legs. There was chocolate pudding all over his shirt.

"We'll see you Thursday?"

"Uh, yeah," Abby said, putting the money in her jeans pocket. "Good-bye, Geoffrey."

"No!" Geoffrey said.

Abby waved to Elaine and ran down the porch steps. The cold air was refreshing on her face. She couldn't wait to get home.

Somehow she had made it through an afternoon with Geoffrey. He'd had only two tantrums, hidden for a mere twenty minutes, and dumped chocolate pudding in her lap only once. After cleaning up the chocolate pudding, she had read his favorite book, *Itty Baby in the Bath*, at least two hundred times.

Now she could recite it by heart, along with Geoffrey:

"Itty Baby in the Bath
Likes to Swim
And do his Math . . .

One, Two, Three, Four,
Itty Baby, count some more!"

"One, two, three, four," Abby recited as she hurried home. "I can't stand Itty Baby anymore!"

Yes, she had gotten through one afternoon. But then there was Thursday . . . and Saturday morning . . . and next Tuesday . . . and the Thursday after. . . .

How had Jessica done it????

She must have Super Sitter powers and chocolate-proof clothes. She could stop terrible tantrums in the blink of an eye. She could leap over couches and see behind doors to find the most well-hidden toddler!

If Jessica were home, Abby would be on the phone with her right now. She would be confiding every detail of her afternoon with Geoffrey. They would be laughing about it together and figuring out what to do next. But Jessica was in Oregon. She wasn't easy to reach.

Why did Jessica have to leave??

"Hey, Hayes! Howdy!"

Only one person in Lancaster Elementary called Abby "Hayes." And only one person would think it was funny to say "howdy."

"Hi, Hoffman," Abby retorted. It wasn't much of

a retort, but after reading *Itty Baby in the Bath* all afternoon, it was the best she could do.

Casey Hoffman was Abby's only friend who was a boy. But he was NOT a boyfriend. (No matter what Brianna said.)

"Urp!" Mason announced his presence with a belch.

Mason was big, bold, and boisterous. He was the one boy Brianna couldn't stand.

"The Big Burper is here," Casey said.

Both boys had rakes in their hands.

"Casey and I have earned fifteen dollars this afternoon," Mason bragged. "That's seven-fifty apiece."

"Plus cookies and apple cider," Casey added. "Do you want to join us raking leaves, Hayes?"

"Leaves, Hayes?" Mason repeated, punctuating his comment with another loud burp. "How about raking Hayes, leaves?"

"That doesn't make any sense," Abby said.

"No," Casey agreed. "Try again, Mason." He winked at Abby.

"Eeerp!" Mason said instead.

"I just earned six dollars," Abby said. "Plus chocolate pudding." She was glad her coat was long. It covered the stains.

"What were you doing?" Casey asked.

"Baby-sitting." Abby pointed to Geoffrey's house. "It's Jessica's job."

"I know that Geoffrey kid," Mason said. "My sister Kathleen baby-sits him on Saturday nights."

"Really?" Abby said. "Does she like him?"

Mason shrugged. "She says he's cute."

"Cute?" Abby repeated. "That's not how — " She stopped. Maybe Kathleen knew how to handle Geoffrey. After all, Mason was her brother.

Once again she wished that Jessica wasn't so far away.

The streetlights flickered and came on.

Casey checked his watch. "I'm late," he said. "My parents don't like me to be out after dark."

"Me, neither," Abby said. She glanced at the sky. "It's not dark yet, but it will be soon."

"We'll walk home together," Casey offered.

Mason brandished his rake. "If anyone tries to bother us . . ."

"You'll burp," Abby finished.

"He's trained himself carefully," Casey told Abby. "Long, lonely years were spent developing his special talent. Now he's the only kid in the fifth grade who can burp on demand."

"Even Brianna is jealous!" Mason cackled.

"Yeah, right," Abby said.

The three fifth-graders walked home under the streetlamps. Newly fallen leaves crackled under their feet. The sidewalk in front of Abby's house was covered with them.

"See you tomorrow in school," Abby said.

"See tomorrow in school, you!" Casey replied.

"Not funny, Hoffman!" Mason slapped him on the back.

"Good-bye!" Abby yelled as she ran up the driveway. It was fun to see Casey and Mason outside of school. But they still weren't Jessica.

Abby rushed into the house. "I'm home!" she called. "I'm back!"

"How did it go?" her mother asked. She was still in her work clothes but wore fuzzy slippers on her feet.

"Well," Abby began. She was dying to tell *someone* about her afternoon.

"Mom!!! Where's my basketball jersey?" Eva demanded, rushing into the room. "I have practice in fifteen minutes!"

"Sorry, Abby. Later," her mother said.

Abby took off her coat and boots and went into the kitchen. "I'm back from my baby-sitting job," she announced.

"Congratulations," her father said. He stirred a pot of tomato sauce. "I hope you didn't walk home alone in the dark."

"I walked home with Mason and Casey. They were raking lawns."

"While they were walking home?" her father teased.

"Dad!" Abby protested.

Her father smiled.

"Aren't you going to ask me how it went?" Abby said.

"How what went?"

"Baby-sitting Geoffrey!!"

Her father gave her a hug. "I'm sure you were wonderful."

"Well," Abby began again. Her father was the perfect person to talk to. He'd have something funny to say and then he'd offer sensible advice. He was almost as good as Jessica.

She took a breath. "Geof — "

Isabel stormed into the kitchen. "Terrible news! I placed third in the history competition. *Third!*"

"Sounds good to me," her father commented. "Especially statewide."

"But I should have been first!" Isabel exclaimed.

"Geoffrey dumped chocolate pudding on my la — " Abby said.

"Abby! This is no time to talk about chocolate pudding!" Isabel cried.

"But Geoffrey — " Abby protested.

"Never mind Geoffrey! This is a tragedy!" Isabel proclaimed, tossing her head dramatically.

Paul Hayes glanced at Abby. "Sorry, honey," he said. "Why don't you tell me all about it later?"

Why did Jessica have to go to Oregon?

Abby wandered into Alex's room. He was reading a book.

"Do you want to hear about my baby-sitting job?" she asked.

He didn't answer.

"I didn't think so," Abby said.

Chapter 6

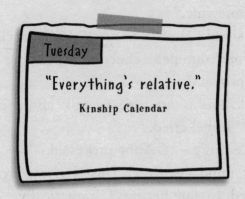

Tuesday

"Everything's relative."

Kinship Calendar

I wish it wasn't! Then it wouldn't bother me so much when my relatives don't have time for me.

Everything's Relative, or Abby's Brief Theory of Relativity

1. Usually I hate homework. After baby-sitting Geoffrey, it's a relief to do homework. (Homework doesn't hide. Or throw chocolate pudding. Or do anything unexpected.)

2. Jessica is far away. When my whole family is too busy to talk to me, she's the closest person around.

Relatively Important Questions

1. How do you get chocolate pudding stains out of clothes?

2. How many times can a person read <u>Itty Baby in the Bath</u> without going insane?

3. Is Mason <u>really</u> as obnoxious as he seems? (Or is he secretly nice?)

4. Why does everyone in my family keep saying, "Sorry, Abby. Later"?

5. When will Jessica answer my e-mail? It's two days since I wrote her. I need more Geoffrey-taming tips! I want to know what she's doing! I need to know if she misses me as much as I miss her!

Wednesday

Still no answer from Jessica. What's happened to her????

a) She is so happy that she's forgotten all about us!

b) She's so unhappy that she's forgotten all about us!

c) She's forgotten all about us! (Out of sight, out of mind? Nooooooo . . .)

My gloomy thoughts are interrupted by a call from Natalie.

Hooray! I can talk to Natalie! She will sympathize with my terrible ordeal.

A Conversation Between Two Friends

Natalie: The movie committee is going to make their decision soon. But first we're polling class members. Do you think we should see <u>Twenty-two Rottweilers</u>? Or <u>The Princess Mermaid</u>? Or <u>Asteroid!</u>? Or <u>The Tiffany Crystal Story</u>?

Abby (dismayed): Those are the choices?

Natalie: Unless you want to see <u>The Aardvark King</u>.

Abby: Ugh.

Natalie: I agree.

Abby: What about <u>Darling, I've Shrink-wrapped My Elbow</u>?

Natalie: No one likes that one.

Abby (desperate): <u>Bub</u>?

Natalie: Are you serious?

Abby: No.

Natalie: Well, what's your choice?

Abby: <u>Secret of the Baby-sitters, Part II</u>.

Natalie: That's a good one. Why don't you come to the meeting tomorrow after school and suggest it?

Abby: I have to watch Geoffrey.

Natalie: Too bad.

Abby: That's for sure.

Natalie: Huh?

Abby (hopeful): It's a long story. Do you want to hear it?

Natalie: Later. I still have half the class to call.

Abby: Never mind. Which movie do you think will win?

Natalie: <u>The Princess Mermaid</u>.

Abby: Does that mean mermaids on the poster?

Natalie: Yes.

Abby: I guess they're better than aardvarks — or Tiffany Crystal.

After I hung up the phone, I checked

my e-mail again. Still nothing from Jessica. Went to find T-Jeff. He was sleeping in the upstairs closet. I petted him until he started to purr.

T-Jeff, you're always my friend! Even when no one else is around.

Thursday noon

Natalie and Sarah and Bethany and I had lunch together.

They asked me if I'd heard from Jessica. I asked _them_ if they had heard from her. None of us had.

What We Talked About

Sarah: Skiing. Now that Jessica is gone, she's looking for another friend to ski with.

Natalie: Movies. Says it's too bad Jessica can't vote for her favorite movie.

Bethany: Pets. Wonders if Dakota and Danielle have any.

Abby: Nothing.

What We Didn't Talk About

Why it isn't any fun to eat lunch together now that Jessica is gone.

Why everyone always talks about the
same thing, over and over.

They argued about movies for the rest of
lunch period. I pretended to listen but was
really thinking about Jessica.

And Geoffrey, of course. I have to
baby-sit him in only a few short hours. I
asked Sarah, Natalie, and Bethany for
advice. They didn't have anything to say.

Jessica _always_ has advice!

Thursday, 3:00 P.M.

Why does school have to end?

Thursday, 3:05 P.M.

Off to meet my doom! Into the House of
Geoffrey. (Good subject for horror movie. Be
sure to suggest it for movie night.)

I have to baby-sit _again_ on Saturday. How did Jessica do it? (She dog walked, too!)

Scene

The fearless fifth-grader with curly red hair puts on her pea coat. With a careless nod to her friends, she winds her striped scarf around her neck. Bravely, she shoulders her backpack.

"Good luck!" Natalie and Bethany call to her. They leave the classroom together, chatting, ignorant of the dangers that their close friend will soon encounter.

Abby walks out of the school alone. She faces into the wind, which is brisk and cold.

"Eeerp!" Mason comes up behind her and tries to startle her.

"Oh, hi, Mason," Abby says. Even world-class burps can't upset her now, when she is on her way to Geoffrey's house.

"Walking this way?" Mason asks.

"Uh-huh," Abby answers. She is deep in thought. She is trying to think of what to do over the next three hours. Dance? Sing? Stand on her head?

She is facing a doom darker and stickier than any known to man, woman, or child.

Suddenly she remembers. Mason's sister has taken care of Geoffrey. "Is Kathleen home?" she asks the Big Burper.

"No," Mason says.

Her last hopes are dashed. Geoffrey's house looms on the corner. The windows gleam with an evil light. . . .

Thursday, 6:35 P.M.

I am still alive!!!!

Not only that, but baby-sitting Geoffrey was okay . . . ???
Can it be true?

Did we really go to the park and have fun on the swings?

Did I only have to read his favorite book three times?

Did he really sulk when I left?

1. Pinch arm to see if dreaming.
2. Call Natalie to announce news. (It doesn't matter if she's not home!)
3. Breathe GIGANTIC sigh of relief!

Am I a natural baby-sitter? Or even a baby-sitting genius, like Jessica? Maybe I'm a Super Sitter, too!

Ha-ha-ha! I did it all myself, without any help from anyone! And I have twelve dollars in my pocket to spend any way I please!

HOORAY!!!

I am saving Jessica's job for her. Can I do it again? And again and again and again?

I have to keep this up.

I must, I must, I must!

(Otherwise, I'm going to need someone to save me from Jessica's job!)

Chapter 7

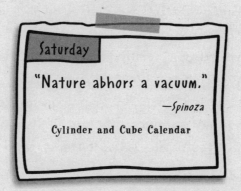

Saturday

"Nature abhors a vacuum."
—Spinoza

Cylinder and Cube Calendar

Does Nature also abhor vacuum cleaners? I do! (Abhor means hate. Thank you, Isabel Hayes, human dictionary.)

I also abhor dust rags, brooms, and ammonia!

In addition, I abhor cleaning my room, especially early on a Saturday morning.

Saturdays should be dedicated to fun!!!!

No responsibilities of any kind. No housework. And no thinking about school – not even about movie night.

(What would my parents say about *No Responsibility Saturdays?* I don't think they'd agree!)

I don't abhor writing in my journal. Or seeing my friends. Or e-mailing them. Jessica <u>finally</u> e-mailed me! She apologized for not answering me sooner.

Geoffrey tests his baby-sitters, she wrote. I hope I passed. I don't want to take the test again.

Jessica is swimming almost every night with Danielle. They have more homework than we do. She sounded really busy. But she said she misses us!

I still miss her, too.

But I can't sit around the house feeling sad and lonely. Three months is a long time. Jessica is having fun with Danielle. I'll have fun with other friends, too! Maybe I'll even make new friends!

Abby gave her bureau a final swipe with the dust rag, sneezed once, and sat down on her bed. The room smelled of lemon polish. The sun shone through the freshly cleaned window.

As Abby stared at the bright purple walls and the calendars that covered them, a knock sounded on her door.

"Abby!" Eva called. "Phone for you."

Abby wiped her hands on her jeans and took the phone. "Hello?"

"Hey, Hayes," Casey said.

"Hi, Hoffman?" Abby replied, in surprise. Casey didn't often call her. "What's up?"

"I have an extra ticket for a college soccer game today. Want to come?"

"Soccer? I love soccer," Abby said.

"It's going to be an exciting match," Casey promised.

"Great! I'll ask my parents. Hold on."

Just a few minutes ago, she had been writing in her journal about doing new things with new people. Here was her chance.

Abby put down the phone and went to look for her mom and dad. She hoped they would say yes. She really wanted to go.

"Dad?" she called. She ran up the stairs to her father's home office. No one was there.

"Eva?" Abby banged at her door. "Where are Mom and Dad?"

Her older sister was doing sit-ups. "I dunno. Somewhere."

Abby ran downstairs.

At the kitchen table, Isabel sat in front of a pile of books. She was taking notes on a laptop computer.

"Where are Mom and Dad?" Abby asked.

"Out," Isabel said vaguely.

"Will they be back soon?"

"I hope so." Isabel tapped a quick sentence onto the screen.

"Casey invited me to a soccer game." Abby frowned at her sister. "Do you think it's okay if I go? I finished cleaning my room."

Isabel looked up from the computer. "Did you do all your homework?"

"I don't have any," Abby said.

"Wait until you get to high school," Isabel promised. "You'll have *hours* of it!"

"Did Mom and Dad leave you in charge?" Abby asked. "Or Eva?"

"Me, of course," Isabel said.

"I have basketball practice." Eva had a gym bag slung over her shoulder. "Otherwise *I'd* be in charge."

Opening the back door, Eva let in a blast of icy air. She smirked at her twin and slammed the door shut.

"Well, what do you think?" Abby demanded. She knew better than to take sides in any argument between her sisters. "Can I go? Casey's waiting."

"Leave a note for Mom and Dad," Isabel said, returning to her work. "Tell them where you are, who you're with, when you'll be back. They know Casey's parents. It should be fine."

"Yay!" Abby cried.

She went back upstairs and picked up the phone. "I can go!" she cried.

Casey sounded pleased. "We'll pick you up in half an hour. Mason's mother is driving."

"Mason's mother?" Abby didn't know her — and neither did her parents. She wondered what they would say. She hoped it would be okay.

"Is Mason coming, too?"

"The Big Burper gave me the tickets," Casey said.

"You sit between us," Abby instructed him.

Abby opened the back door of the car. Casey was sitting next to the window. In the front sat Mason and his mother.

"Hello, I'm Betsy," Mason's mother said. She was a large woman with a booming voice. "Are you Abby?"

"Uh-huh," Abby said. She slid into the seat next to Casey. "Nice to meet you."

"Don't say that!" Betsy warned, adjusting the headset of her cell phone. "It might not be nice to meet me."

"Yes, it is!" Casey protested.

"Uurrrp," Mason said.

"I knew you were going to say that," Abby said.

"He's so predictable," Betsy said. The cell phone rang. The ringer had been set to play "Happy Birthday."

"Hello? Hello?" Betsy said. She punched some buttons, then sighed. "Hung up. Wrong number."

"Is it someone's birthday?" Abby asked.

"Nope," Betsy said cheerfully. "I just like the tune." She fiddled with the radio dial. "What kind of music do you like, Abby? Country and western? Oldies? Tiffany Crystal? Opera?"

It was exciting to be on her way to a soccer match with different friends, Abby thought. She enjoyed being with boys for a change. And meeting Mason's mom, too.

"I like the Bumble Boys," Abby said to Betsy.

"They're the worst!" Mason cried.

"Thank you for making my son speak," Betsy said

to Abby. "I thought we were in the middle of a record-breaking burp-a-thon."

The cell phone rang again. The happy birthday tune jingled.

"Hello?" Betsy yelled. "Was that just you?"

In the backseat, Abby and Casey exchanged grins.

"Mason, I'll put you in *The Hayes Book of World Records* for Biggest and Best Burping," Abby offered. "You'll get your own page."

"Oh, wow," Mason said, punctuating his comment with yet another burp.

"That wasn't Biggest and Best," Betsy complained, switching off the phone. "Don't disappoint your friends."

"We're not disappointed!" Abby cried.

"Hayes speaks for us all," Casey said.

Betsy turned into a parking lot. "We're here because we're here because we're . . ."

The phone rang again.

"Enough is enough," Betsy announced.

"Eerp!" Mason said.

The fifth-graders piled out of the car.

"Go right over there!" Betsy ordered them. "Show your tickets, and get good seats! That's a command!"

Abby followed Mason. She was having more fun

than she had had in a while. Maybe it was even better than *before* Jessica had left.

Mason handed over the tickets and the three fifth-graders climbed into the bleachers together.

As they left the stadium a few hours later, a brisk wind blew up. Abby wound her scarf more tightly around her neck. She was glad she had worn her winter coat and gloves.

"Wasn't that a great game, Hayes?" Casey said.

"I loved it," she replied. "It was exciting when they scored the winning goal at the last minute!"

"The goalie just missed the ball," Mason said. "His teammates must be mad at him!"

"There's your mother," Abby said, pointing to Betsy. She stood in front of her car, gesturing to the fifth-graders.

"Hurry up!" she yelled. "It's freezing!"

As they dashed toward the car, brightly colored leaves fluttered to the ground.

"It's leaf-raking weather," Casey commented. "We have twelve jobs lined up for next week. More than the two of us can rake."

"We're going to make a pile of money!" Mason said gleefully. "Enough to jump in!"

"Well, I made twelve dollars last week," Abby bragged. "Just from baby-sitting Geof — "

She stopped suddenly.

Mason opened the car door for his friends. "Get in!"

They piled into the car.

"How was the game?" Betsy asked in a loud, cheerful voice.

"Awesome," Mason said, punching the air.

"Awfully awesome," Casey added. "Amazingly awesome! Agree, Abby?"

Abby shook her head. Even though Casey had called her Abby for the first time in history, she still couldn't say a word.

"What's the matter?" Betsy frowned. She turned the key in the ignition.

"Is the goalie your brother?" Mason asked.

Abby pointed to Casey's watch.

"It's one o'clock," Casey said. "Are you okay, Hayes?"

"No," Abby whispered. "I'm not. I was supposed to baby-sit Geoffrey at ten o'clock this morning. I forgot all about it."

Chapter 8

Saturday afternoon

"And we forget because
we must and not because
we will."

—*Matthew Arnold*
Responsible Reminder Calendar

<u>Must</u> I have forgotten about baby-sitting Geoffrey this morning?

1. I wrote down the date on five different calendars. (But I forgot to check them.)
2. Isabel asked me if I was done with my work. I said yes. (But I forgot about baby-sitting work.)
3. Mom and Dad might have reminded me about it. (But they weren't here.)

Conclusion

I didn't want to forget! (But I did!)

Painful Questions
Did I forget because I needed to have fun with Mason and Casey?

Did I forget because I _did_ have fun with Mason and Casey? (And Betsy, too.)

More Painful Questions
What will happen when I get home? What will Elaine say? What will Mom and Dad say? What will Jessica say? What will _I_ say?

Jessica will be _so_ angry! She never forgets anything. She's always responsible, always on time, and always organized.

She won't understand how I forgot about Geoffrey.

Why does my best friend have to be per-fect . . . like the rest of my family!!!

Abby climbed out of the car.

"Thanks for the ride," she said to Betsy. "Thanks for inviting me," she said to Mason and Casey.

"Good luck," Betsy said. "We all make mistakes."

Abby took a deep breath. She didn't think her parents would say that. Both cars were in the garage. She wondered if Elaine had called and talked to them.

"Don't worry, Hayes," Casey said.

"Eeerp," Mason added. "Just trying to cheer you up," he explained.

Abby waved good-bye and walked slowly up the driveway.

The front door opened. It was Alex. His hair stuck straight up, as if he had glued it.

"Abby!" he said. "Jessica called from Oregon!"

"Jessica!!!????" Abby cried. "Did you talk to her? How is she? What did she say?"

"She said hi," Alex said.

"That's *it*? Hi?"

"And don't call her; she's going ice-skating with Danielle."

"Oh." Disappointed, Abby shut the front door behind her. She hung her coat in the closet and kicked off her boots. "Will she call me back?"

"If she has time," Alex said. He picked up the cordless phone. "Peter's going to call me soon."

"Sure," Abby said. She walked into the living room. "Anyone else call?"

Alex shrugged. "Ask Mom."

She sat down on the couch. Maybe it was just as well that she had missed Jessica's call. What would she have said? *Guess what? I forgot all about Geoffrey today.*

Now she had to call Elaine. That was going to be hard, too. What was she going to tell her? *Going to a soccer game with Mason and Casey was more exciting than baby-sitting, so I forgot. . . .*

"Give me the phone," she said to Alex, holding out her hand.

"Jessica won't be home," he repeated.

"I *know*!" Abby said irritably.

"Grump," Alex said. He tossed it into her lap. "Don't be long. I'm waiting for Peter."

Abby stared at the phone. She picked it up and dialed the first five digits of Elaine's phone number. Then she pressed the OFF button.

She dialed again and hung up.

And again.

She couldn't do it.

She replaced the phone on its cradle and went to find her mother.

Her mother was in the kitchen, emptying the dishwasher. She frowned when she saw Abby.

"Elaine called," she said.

"I'm sorry!" Abby cried. "I forgot!!!"

"She had an important project to finish. She was counting on you."

"Sorry!" Abby said again.

Her mother continued. "She couldn't find another baby-sitter to replace you. Isabel offered to go over there."

Abby flushed red. Not only had she messed up, but her older sister had saved the day. How much worse could it get?

"I think Isabel should take over baby-sitting Geoffrey until Jessica gets back," her mother finished.

"*What???*" Abby cried. "That's not fair!!"

Her mother shook her head. "If you're not responsible enough to show up at your job, why should she keep you?"

Abby stared at her mother in dismay. This was a disaster.

"It was just once! Just one little mistake," Abby

pleaded. "And I'm really sorry. I'll never do it again."

"Sorry isn't enough. Elaine needs a reliable baby-sitter. If you go off to a soccer game with your friends, what's she supposed to do?"

"I get the point," Abby muttered.

She had known that everyone would be mad, but she never thought she'd lose the job. How could she ever tell Jessica?

Her mother put away the last clean dish.

"You owe Elaine an apology and Isabel a thank-you," she said. "I'm disappointed in you, Abby."

Abby went to her room and sat on the bed. For once, the bright purple walls failed to cheer her up.

She picked up her journal, then put it down.

The phone rang. She picked it up and pressed the ON button.

"Hello," she muttered into the receiver.

"Abby, it's Natalie! Where have you been?"

"Out," Abby said in a depressed voice. Natalie didn't seem to notice.

"I've been calling you all morning and getting a busy signal. Guess what?"

Abby sighed.

"We finally decided on a movie last night after school," Natalie announced. "It was a surprise win for *Merlin's Magic School*!"

"A fantasy?"

"Yep," Natalie said.

"How did you get everyone to vote for it?" Abby asked.

"A lot of kids wanted it." Natalie paused dramatically. "And Brianna made a speech in favor of it."

"Brianna??"

"Brianna's mother's aunt's third cousin's husband's sister-in-law has a cameo role in *Merlin's Magic School*."

"Oh, wow," Abby said.

"We're going to serve donuts and cider and call them Dragon Rings and Toad's Blood," Natalie continued. "Brianna suggested we all come in costume."

"Brianna will be a toad?" Abby asked hopefully.

"She's planning to dress as a sorceress."

"An evil one," Abby said. "And you'll be Merlin."

"Of course!" Natalie agreed.

"What about me?" Abby asked. "Who will I be?

One of the apprentices?"

"If you want. You don't *have* to come in costume," Natalie reassured her. "All you have to do is get the posters out."

"Oh, right, the posters," Abby mumbled. She didn't feel like thinking about them right now.

"We'll have huge crowds!" Natalie cried. "Once we get the word out, every kid under twelve will want to come. Be sure to put them all over town!"

"How long do I have?"

"Ten days. We have to have them up at least a week before movie night."

"Okay." Abby sighed deeply. "I have other things on my mind today."

"Like what?" Natalie asked.

"Stuff," Abby replied. She changed the subject. "Too bad Jessica's going to miss the movie."

"I think she's having fun in Oregon," Natalie said.

"Did you talk to her?" Abby cried eagerly. "How is she?"

"She's going to a dance party."

"A dance party? *Jessica?*"

"Yep," Natalie said.

"Did she say anything about me?"

"We only talked for five minutes," Natalie said. "I told her about the dogs. How was Geoffrey today?"

"He was . . . uh — "

"Do you need help with the posters?" Natalie interrupted.

"No, thanks. I'll start working on them this weekend. Geoffrey was — " Abby tried again and stopped. "I — "

She couldn't say another word. It was too painful.

"I've got to go," Natalie said. "Bethany and I are going out for ice cream. Want to come?"

"No money," Abby said. She had spent most of it this morning at the soccer game and she wouldn't be earning more in the future. Her parents wouldn't be handing her any cash, either. Not after today.

"Maybe another time," Natalie said.

"Maybe," Abby repeated.

Maybe another time she'd tell Natalie what had happened.

"Good-bye," she said glumly. She hung up the phone.

The walls of her room were just as purple. The calendars were just as numerous. Nothing had changed. Except now, on top of everything else, she had a poster to think about.

It would have to be a magnificent poster: exciting, dramatic, and irresistible. A poster that would prove she knew how to do *something* right. Maybe she'd use glitter pens and stickers on each one.

She didn't have any money to buy supplies, though.

Abby felt even worse than she had before Natalie called.

Chapter 9

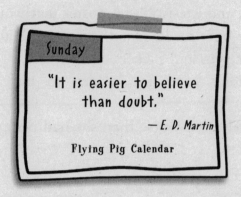

For my best friend, it is easier to doubt than believe.

Jessica found out what happened and wrote me a long e-mail. She was very upset.

<u>Jessica doubts</u>

1. that Abby can hold down a job.

2. that Abby can remember she has a job.

3. that Abby is responsible and mature.

4. that Abby cares about her friends.

My best friend has lost trust in me!!!!!!!!

So has Elaine. She told Isabel that Jessica had given me an excellent recommendation. She was disappointed and angry when I didn't show up. I have lost my baby-sitting job, Jessica's trust, and Elaine's confidence.

(We pause for a moment of quiet despair.)

What to Do, Part One

1. Cry quietly in my room for ten minutes.
2. Get up, blow nose, and wipe eyes.
3. Look at face in mirror.
4. Decide to go out and get fresh air.
5. Try to avoid seeing anyone as I slip out of the house.
6. Walk along the streets, kicking at fallen leaves.
7. Feel miserable and alone.
8. Wish for someone

to wave a magic wand and change my life completely.

9. Not pay any attention to where I'm going or who's near me.

10. Bump into a large body who yelps in surprise.

Life, Limb, and Leaf
A true story by Abby Hayes

"Watch it!" Mason yelled.

"Sorry!" the distressed fifth-grader apologized. "I didn't see you."

"Did you have your eyes closed?" Casey asked. "No one can miss Mason."

"I'm unmissable," bragged the Mason Man.

"Did I hurt you?" she asked, feeling even worse than before. On top of everything else, she was crashing into innocent bystanders.

"Eeerp," Mason burped. "I've got too many layers on." He waved a puffy, down-filled sleeve in the air.

"We've been working all afternoon," Casey

explained, holding up a rake. "It's chilly today."

"I guess," Abby said. The wind blew her curly red hair into her face. She pushed it away with numb fingers.

"Wasn't the soccer game great yesterday?" Mason said.

Abby sighed tragically. "It's because of that soccer game that everyone's mad at me."

Casey raked some leaves into a pile. "What? For missing baby-sitting once?"

"Kathleen forgets things all the time!" Mason said. "Her homework, her gym clothes, her contact lenses, her brain."

"Neither of my sisters forgets anything, ever. They're so responsible that no one would even believe it if they messed up!" Abby cried. "And Jessica's the same way!"

"Gee, that's too bad," Mason said sympathetically.

"It won't happen again," Casey reassured her. "For the rest of your life, you'll never, ever forget a baby-sitting date. My mother says all you need is one big mistake to learn from."

Abby looked down at the ground. "I don't get a second chance," she said miserably. "Elaine fired me and hired my sister instead."

"That stinks!" Mason yelled.

"Yeah," Casey agreed.

"Jessica is furious, too. She thinks I'm irresponsible," Abby concluded. "How can I show her that I'm not?"

Casey leaned his rake against a tree. "Ask Geoffrey's mother to give you another try."

"_No!_" Abby cried. "Never!"

Mason belched loudly.

"Is that your suggestion for Abby?" Casey asked.

Mason brandished his rake in the air. "Why don't you rake leaves with us? We have more work than we can handle."

"That won't prove anything to Jessica," she said.

"You'll earn money," Casey pointed out. "And have fun with me and the Mason Man."

Abby sniffed and wiped her nose. She rubbed her two cold hands together and drew her scarf tighter around her neck.

She needed money. She really needed fun.

"When do I start?" she asked.

What to Do, Part Two

1. Run home.

2. Change into warmer clothes. Put on down jacket and fleece hat. Find winter gloves.

3. Run into kitchen.

4. Announce to mother that I will be raking leaves with Casey and Mason all afternoon.

5. Agree to be home before dark.

6. Leave before anyone can say a word about yesterday.

Chapter 10

Friday morning

"Promise, large promise,
is the soul of an
advertisement."
—Samuel Johnson

Great Big Calendar of Soup Labels

Or the soul of a poster.

<u>What my poster will promise</u>

1. A movie full of adventure and magic
2. Delicious refreshments
3. Costumes and entertainment.
4. Money donated to charity

Are these large enough promises? Will they make everyone want to come to the Silver Screen Savers movie night??

What my poster will look like

1. Bright fluorescent colors: green, pink, turquoise, and coral
2. Big lettering
3. Bold illustrations of stars and donuts (Dragon Rings). (I hope the Dragon Rings don't look like breakfast cereal!)
4. Glittery designs and rainbow stickers

Mom and I bought supplies for the poster on Wednesday. I earned enough money from raking leaves for plenty of pens and stickers! I designed the poster on the computer last night and printed a few out.

Maybe I'll get one of my friends to look at the poster before I distribute it. I want it to be _perfect_!!!

Tomorrow Dad will drive me around to put it up in stores, schools, and on bulletin boards all over the city. Then I'll call the local radio and television stations.

By the end of the weekend, the entire city will be lining up to buy tickets for the Silver Screen Savers movie night!!

"Have you heard anything from Jessica?" Natalie asked Abby as they left Lancaster Elementary at the end of the day.

The two girls were on their way to Abby's house to look at the movie-night poster.

"Not lately," Abby said, adjusting the straps of her backpack. It wasn't exactly a lie. She hadn't heard from Jessica since last weekend.

"Jessica hasn't written or called me, either," Sarah chimed in, joining them as they crossed the playground.

"Is it us? Or is it her?" Abby asked. She had been worrying all week because Jessica hadn't responded to her note of apology.

"Dunno." Sarah shrugged.

"We should send an electronic greeting from the three of us," Natalie said. "Something funny."

"Great idea!" Sarah said. She pulled a red-patterned ski cap over her curly brown hair.

Abby didn't say anything.

"Have a good weekend, girls!" Ms. Yang, the principal, stood on the playground, watching the students leave.

"Thanks, Ms. Yang!" Natalie said.

The three girls strolled down the street.

"Why don't we send a greeting to Jessica right now?" Natalie suggested. "We'll use Abby's computer. Want to come with us, Sarah?"

"Yes!" Sarah said enthusiastically. She turned to Abby. "Okay?"

"Uh, sure, okay." Abby wished that Natalie had asked her first before inviting Sarah to *her* house.

Natalie skipped a few feet ahead, then faced the two girls. "Sarah, you can help us with the poster, too. Abby wants feedback. Right, Abby?"

"Right," Abby muttered. Did she have a choice? Natalie was making all the decisions.

Sarah rummaged in her pockets and pulled out a stick of gum. "Do you have snacks at your house?" she asked Abby.

"The usual boring stuff," Abby said. "Granola bars, graham crackers, cheese puffs."

"I love cheese puffs!" Sarah said, unwrapping the gum and putting it in her mouth.

The three girls turned down Abby's street.

Abby looked up as bright crimson leaves fluttered down from a maple tree. "More raking to do," she said.

"Was that you with Mason and Casey last week?" Sarah asked Abby.

Abby nodded.

She had spent most of her afternoons that week working. She, Casey, and Mason had each made twenty dollars. They had been treated to cookies, hot chocolate, and orange juice. They had gotten lots of exercise and met some friendly neighbors.

Once she saw Elaine and Geoffrey walking down the street together. Abby had hidden behind a tree until they passed.

Mason and Casey teased her about it for the rest of the afternoon.

Automatically, Abby glanced around to see if the boys were raking today. She wondered if they had any extra jobs and if they'd call her.

"You were raking leaves with *MasonandCasey*?" Natalie cried. She pronounced their names as if they were one word.

"Yep." Abby ran up the porch stairs and unlocked the front door of her house.

"But they're — they're — " For once Natalie was at a loss for words.

"Boys?" Abby finished.

"Disgusting boys," Natalie said. "Especially Mason."

"Casey is really nice," Abby protested. "And so is Mason. Once you get to know him. And his mom is so funny."

"Ugh," Natalie said.

Sarah made a face. "I can't stand Casey. He always makes stupid jokes."

Abby slammed the front door shut. The three girls dropped their backpacks in the hallway.

Natalie took off her jacket and walked into the living room. "Which computer are we using?"

"The downstairs one."

"Let's get a snack first," Sarah said.

"Is that all you think about?" Natalie asked.

"Yes!" Sarah retorted.

"The cheese puffs are in the kitchen cupboard," Abby said to Natalie. "Eat all you want."

Abby pointed them in the direction of the kitchen and went to find a poster for them to see.

A few minutes later, the three girls sat around the kitchen table. Abby had taped a fluorescent green poster on the wall above the table.

Natalie and Sarah studied it.

"So? What do you think?" Abby asked.

"You forgot to put the time on it," Natalie said.

"I did?" Abby cried. She jumped up and scrutinized the poster. "I *did*!"

Natalie took a handful of cheese puffs and put them in her mouth. Orange cheese dust covered her lips.

"Mfooellionto," she said.

"Don't talk with your mouth full!" Sarah said.

"I mean, that's easy to fix," Natalie said.

She pointed to the poster. "And don't forget to say that refreshments will be served by fifth-graders in costumes!"

"I won't — I mean — I *didn't* forget," Abby said.

"Make the donuts larger," Natalie continued. "They look like breakfast cereal."

"Breakfast cereal?" Abby repeated. "Why not rings or halos?"

Natalie didn't reply. "The title of the movie should be larger," she said. "Can you put it into fancy type? Like calligraphy?"

"I guess," Abby said.

Natalie grabbed another handful of cheese puffs.

"Save some for me!" Sarah cried. "Don't hog them all!"

"Pleckifooey," Natalie mumbled, spewing more orange cheese dust on her face. "There's plenty for everyone."

Abby nibbled on a pretzel and studied her poster. It didn't need *that* much work. Or did it?

"It's time to e-mail Jessica," Natalie suddenly announced.

"Yes!" Sarah cried. She scooped up the final handful of cheese puffs.

"You took the last ones!" Natalie protested.

"Who pigged out just now?" Sarah demanded, eating the cheese puffs one by one.

"Come on, everyone," Abby said. "Cheese puffs aren't the most important thing in the world."

She sounded stuffy and grown-up, like a parent or teacher. Why was she so out of tune with her friends?

"Yes, they *are*!" Sarah and Natalie chimed in unison.

The two girls began to laugh. Sarah offered Natalie the last few puffs.

"These cheese puffs are slimy!" Natalie shrieked.

Sarah shrugged and popped them into her mouth.

Natalie stood up. She dusted off her hands and threw the crumpled bag into the garbage.

"Time to send the card," she announced again.

Sarah jumped up.

Abby glanced at her poster one last time. When she made all the changes, would the poster be so exciting and beautiful that people would rush to see the movie?

Maybe it still needed extra glitter. Or magic wizard stickers. Or colored markers, or —

Natalie tapped Abby on the shoulder. "Let's go!"

The three girls went to the computer to send the electronic greeting to Jessica. They logged on to an e-card site.

Natalie took charge again.

"This one," she said. Natalie clicked on the image of a barking dog, then wrote "Wish you were here!" and signed all of their names.

"What about a rainbow?" Sarah suggested.

"No," Natalie said.

She never used to be like this, Abby thought. Was it because Jessica was gone?

Natalie pointed to another card that had planets

revolving in a starry sky. It said, "You're out of this world!"

"Perfect!" Sarah cried. "Don't you think so, Abby?"

"Uh, yeah," Abby said.

Everything had changed in only a few short weeks. Natalie was bossy, Sarah was hanging around too much, Jessica wasn't speaking to her. . . .

Abby didn't know who her friends were anymore — or whether she even had any.

Chapter 11

Saturday

"Be busy and you will
be safe."

—Ovid

Daily Match Calendar

My parents must be <u>very</u> safe! Because they are busier than anyone I know!

My dad:
1. Has to finish rush project.
2. Has to shop and do errands.
3. Has to bring car in for repair.
4. Is going out of town tomorrow with Eva to watch tournament.

My mom:
1. Has to review case for Monday court appearance.

2. Has her turn to carpool for Alex's chess club.

3. Must do week's worth of laundry.

4. Will entertain friends tonight at our house.

The only time Dad can take me out to distribute the posters is between eleven and twelve today. I have to knock on his office door at ten to eleven. He's leaving the house at eleven.

The posters are printed out and deco-rated with glitter and stickers. There's a rainbow-colored stack of them on my desk. After I'm done plastering them all over town, I'm going to rake leaves again with Mason and Casey!

That'll be more fun than spending time after school with my girlfriends! At least the boys don't boss me around!

Isabel and Eva are also busy. Eva is at a practice (surprise!). Isabel is baby-sitting for Geoffrey this morning (boohoo).

Last night, Mom asked me if I had apologized to Elaine yet.

"Uh, no, not really," I mumbled.

Mom just looked at me.

I couldn't say another word.

My room is clean and my Saturday morning chores are done. It's 10:25 A.M. I will offer to help her with the laundry. She'll find out that I'm <u>not</u> irresponsible and forgetful!

"Take the clothes out of the dryer and fold and sort them," Olivia Hayes told Abby.

"Should I put them in the laundry basket?" Abby asked.

"Sure," her mother replied. "Then we'll take them upstairs." She sorted through the dirty clothing in the hamper, then looked at Abby.

"Thanks for helping, hon. It's not often that I have volunteers to do laundry. No one enjoys it."

"I do!" Abby said, folding a pair of Eva's Lycra shorts and putting them on a pile of clothing. "Except when I'm down here all alone."

Her mother glanced around the basement. "It's gloomy and damp, isn't it?" She smiled. "It's much more fun with someone to talk to." She began throwing dark clothes into the machine.

"Jessica's mom puts everything in at once," Abby commented. "Lights and darks together."

Olivia Hayes shook her head. "I'd never do that. But then there are six of us and only two of them. They probably don't have much laundry."

"Now she has even less," Abby said.

"Have you heard from Jessica?" Olivia Hayes asked. "Does she like her father's family?"

"Uh . . . she's been too busy to write," Abby said quickly.

"I hope she's writing to her mother."

"She's in Greece," Abby said. "Remember?"

Her mother sighed. "Lucky woman."

She turned the dial on the washing machine. "Do you want to put the soap in?" she asked Abby.

"Yes!" Abby picked up the bottle and filled the cap with liquid detergent. Then she poured it into the machine.

She shut the lid. "Can I start the washing machine?" she asked.

Her mother nodded. "Pull the dial out."

Water began rushing into the machine. Abby went back to the dryer to finish folding clothes. Now her mother would really think that she was responsible and mature.

Her mother pulled out the lint screen to clean it. "Abby, don't avoid apologizing to Elaine," she said.

"Why?" Abby burst out. "Isabel took my place!"

"It's important to face up to your actions. Taking responsibility will give you strength," her mother said.

"It will?" Abby said doubtfully. She hadn't gotten any strength from apologizing to Jessica. She hadn't even gotten any answer!

"Yes," her mother said. "You'll see what happens when you do talk to Elaine."

"I don't want to — " Abby began, and then stopped. She *did* want to be responsible. She wanted her mother to be proud of her. She didn't want her mother to look at her in that disappointed way.

"Okay," she said. "I'll talk to her."

Abby and her mother climbed up the stairs to the kitchen, their arms laden with piles of neatly folded clothes. In the basement, the washing machine was churning out its last load.

"Where do I put these clothes?" Abby asked.

"Bring Eva's and Isabel's up to their rooms," her mother said. "I'll take care of the rest." She put a stack of dish towels on the countertop. "Thanks, Abby! You've been a great help."

Abby smiled. Now her mother would know that she was someone who could be counted on.

"Your help couldn't have come at a better time," her mother continued. "Your father and I are so busy today!"

"Yes, you are," Abby agreed, then suddenly yelled, "*Busy?* Oh, no! What time is it?"

Her mother glanced at her watch. "It's eleven-twenty," she said.

"But we were only downstairs for twenty minutes!" Abby cried.

"No, it was almost an hour," her mother said.

Her arms still full of folded clothes, Abby rushed upstairs. "Dad! Dad!"

She banged on his office door. Shorts and socks fell to the floor.

"Dad????"

Abby dumped Isabel's clothes in a pile on her bed. She left Eva's on her desk. Then she ran back downstairs.

"Where's Dad? Mom, do you know where he is?"

"I think he's out," her mother said. "The car is gone."

"*No!!!*" Abby cried.

"Is something wrong?" her mother asked.

Abby shook her head. She wasn't going to tell her mother she had forgotten to do something important again.

"Can you drive me around later?" she asked. "I need to put up some posters for movie night."

"Not today," her mother said. "Not tomorrow, either. I won't be able to do it until Wednesday."

"That's too late," Abby said.

"Ask your father," her mother said. "He'll help you."

"Sure, Mom," Abby said.

She went back to her room and looked at the pile of posters on her desk. What was she going to do now?

Chapter 12

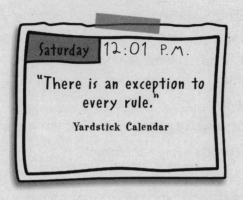

Saturday 12:01 P.M.

"There is an exception to every rule."

Yardstick Calendar

The Rule

Abby forgets!!!!

The Exception

Hasn't shown up yet.
I wish it would.
I need it. I need it <u>now</u>!!!

How could I forget something this important AGAIN??? (Also on a Saturday morning. Is there something dangerous about Saturday mornings?)

Why I Forgot

1. I am wasting away with a mysterious brain disease that causes me to forget only essential and urgent things.

2. Aliens are beaming forgetful rays into my mind.

3. It's the water.

4. I forget why I forgot.

(Will put self in <u>Hayes Book of World Records</u> for Worst Excuses for Worst Behavior.)

Help! Help! <u>Help!</u>

Am I <u>really</u> hopeless? Will I <u>always</u> forget everything important???
OR . . .
Am I caught in a web of mistakes?

Abby's Domino Mistake Theory

1st Mistake: I forget about Geoffrey.

2nd Mistake: So I try to impress my mother.

3rd Mistake: So I miss my appointment with my father.

4th Mistake: So the posters don't get out.

5th Mistake: Yet to come . . .

Conclusion

A single mistake will lead to many others.

What next???

How do I stop the mistakes from happening??? How do I stop being forgetful? How do I start getting the posters up???

My father is busy for the rest of the weekend.

My mother is busy for the rest of the weekend.

No one can drive me to stores and schools where I need to put them up.

Will anyone come to movie night if the posters aren't out?

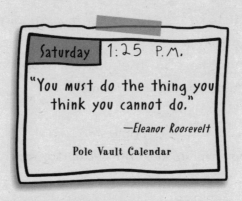

Saturday 1:25 P.M.

"You must do the thing you think you cannot do."

—Eleanor Roosevelt

Pole Vault Calendar

Drive a car????????

Other Solutions

1. Call a taxi (too expensive!).
2. Call someone else's parents and ask them (too embarrassing!).

3. Walk downtown by myself (too hard, too dangerous!).
4. Ask my friends to help distribute the posters.
   a) Casey
   b) Mason (maybe)
   c) Natalie (can't admit what I've done)
   d) Bethany (obsessed with hamsters)

e) Jessica (in Oregon)

f) Brianna (forget it!)

g) Victoria (are you out of your mind?)

h) Sarah (naaaah...)

i) I'm running out of friends

Casey is my only hope.

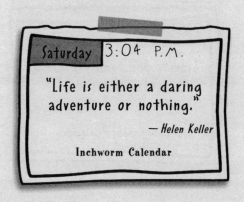

Saturday 3:04 P.M.

"Life is either a daring adventure or nothing."

— Helen Keller

Inchworm Calendar

<u>Yes!</u> I am about to embark on a daring adventure, thanks to Casey.

He suggested I turn the poster into a flyer.

I am printing out hundreds of copies right now.

Casey and I will distribute them to the entire neighborhood.

Hooray! Hooray! I <u>will</u> let people know about the Silver Screen Savers movie night. The school will be packed! We will raise lots of money for the relief fund. Our evening will be a success!

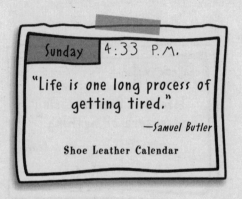

Sunday   4:33 P.M.

"Life is one long process of getting tired."

—Samuel Butler

Shoe Leather Calendar

Flyers distributed: 467
Posters posted: 8
Pairs of shoes worn out: 2
Aching toes: 20 (mine and Casey's)
Grateful friends: 1 (me)

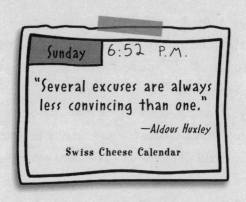

"Several excuses are always
less convincing than one."

—Aldous Huxley

Swiss Cheese Calendar

Are ten excuses more convincing than
two?

Or are two excuses more convincing than
ten?

Is one excuse less convincing than <u>none</u>?

Are <u>all</u> excuses not convincing?

<u>No Excuse! A Phone Conversation</u>

The phone rings. Abby picks it up. It's
Natalie.

Natalie: Hi, Abby!

Abby: Hi!

Natalie: Bethany and I were downtown
today at the pet store. I got a new hamster cage for Madame Curie.

Abby: What color?

Natalie: Blue. (pauses for a moment) Bethany and I looked for posters, but we didn't see any.

Abby: Casey and I went door-to-door yesterday and today. We distributed almost five hundred flyers to the entire neighborhood.

Natalie: I still think we need the posters. What about the people who don't live in our neighborhood?

Abby (looks down at her sore feet): Oh, yeah. Right.

Natalie: Are you going to get them up soon?

Abby: I don't know. My parents are really busy.

Natalie: Bethany and I could have done a lot of them today. You should have asked us!

Abby is too embarrassed to reply. Natalie is right.

Natalie: Do you want us to take some?

Abby: No, no, it's okay. Don't worry — they'll be out by tomorrow.

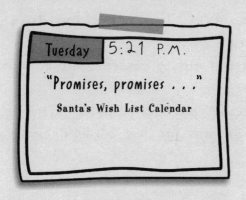

Tuesday   5:21 P.M.

"Promises, promises . . ."

Santa's Wish List Calendar

Promises I Made

1. That two dozen posters (at least!) would be tacked to bulletin boards and community notice boards by tonight.

2. That every supermarket in town would have a poster advertising the Silver Screen Savers movie night.

3. That I would call the local radio and television stations and ask them to broadcast the news about our fund-raiser!

Promises I Kept

1. I called the radio and television stations. Both said I called too late. Even if I had called last weekend, it would have

been too late. They need ten days' advance notice!

2. I put up a poster at our local supermarket.

3. Isabel put up a poster at the library; Eva took one for the athletic center at the college.

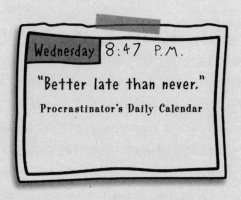

Wednesday 8:47 P.M.

"Better late than never."
Procrastinator's Daily Calendar

The posters are FINALLY! up all over town. Dad was FINALLY! able to drive me around after school. We FINALLY! put them up in supermarkets, schools, drugstores, and gymnasiums.

The Silver Screen Savers movie night is

only two days away. That might not be enough time for people to see the posters.

I might have put them up too late. Late is sometimes NOT better than never.

Late is sometimes equal to never.

P.S. Don't let Natalie know. She thinks the posters went up on Monday.

Chapter 13

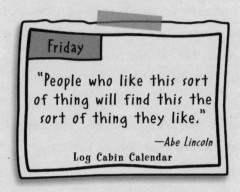

Friday

"People who like this sort of thing will find this the sort of thing they like."

—Abe Lincoln

Log Cabin Calendar

Our Silver Screen Savers movie night <u>will be</u> "the sort of thing people like"!

The Dough Re Mi Bakery has donated Dragon Rings (donuts) and Toad's Blood (cider).

We're also selling Wizard Bricks (brownies), Gobbles (popcorn), and Merlin's Brew (hot chocolate).

We will show cartoons, followed by the feature film.

Ms. Kantor's class will come dressed as characters from <u>Merlin's Magic School</u>.

I am an enchanted pen. I'm
wearing a long purple robe with
gold swirls, and my headpiece is
a pen nib made of aluminum foil
and duct tape.

Everything will be perfect.
Our class has spent weeks preparing for
this event.

Or almost perfect . . .
What if only two or three people show
up?
What if no one eats the donuts, drinks
the cider, or watches the movie?
What if we don't make any money to
donate to the relief fund?

It will all be MY fault!!!!

As the van turned into the Lancaster Elementary
school parking lot, Abby adjusted the silver mask
over her eyes.

She wished that she could turn herself into a real

enchanted pen and write herself into another story.

Her father pulled into a parking spot and turned off the ignition. "You look very nice, honey," he said to Abby.

"Yeah," Abby mumbled. "Thanks."

"Do pens wear sneakers?" her father teased, pointing to the ones peeking out from underneath Abby's robe. "Did they have sneakers in Merlin's time?"

"Merlin used duct tape in his spells," Abby said.

"I forgot about that," her father said.

Abby pulled the robe up around her ankles and stepped out of the car. She glanced anxiously around the parking lot.

The lot was almost empty. What if not even two or three people showed up? What if *no one* showed up?

Slowly she walked toward the school.

"Abby!" Natalie called. She was wearing magician's robes and a tall, pointed hat. She had a wand in one hand and a book of magic spells in the other.

"You look great!" Abby cried.

"You, too," Natalie said. "What are you?"

"An enchanted pen," Abby said.

"You have the 'write' costume, Hayes," Casey said, coming up to them.

"Very punny, Hoffman," Abby retorted, forgetting her worries for a moment.

"Urp." A familiar-sounding burp echoed in the playground.

Abby turned around. Her mouth dropped open. "Is that . . . *Mason*?"

"Urp," he responded.

"Omigosh!" Natalie cried.

For once, even Casey was speechless.

Mason was wearing a black tuxedo with a pink shirt and a bow tie. His hair was slicked back from his face, and his shoes were shining.

"Urp," he said again.

"Could you repeat that, please?" Casey said. He held up his hand. "Just kidding. Don't say another word — or burp."

"You look like a butler," Natalie said.

"I'm an usher!" Mason muttered. "I'm going to take tickets and show the crowds into the gym."

"Crowds?" Abby repeated anxiously. "There aren't any."

"Just wait," Mason said, flinging out his arms. "We'll have to turn them away! We'll have to schedule another showing! We'll —"

"Mason!" Ms. Kantor cried. "We're waiting for

you." Her eyes widened. "Wow," she said. "Wowee."

"Cute!" Bethany squealed. She was dressed in her Halloween hamster costume.

Mason blushed.

"Come in, everyone!" Ms. Kantor said. "We still have plenty to do before the movie starts."

The fifth-graders hurried into the school.

Ms. Kantor gave out orders. "Abby, go in the gym and set up chairs. Natalie, check the refreshment table, and make sure the coffeemaker is plugged in. Bethany, find some tape to put up these signs."

"I'll help," Casey offered.

"Great!" Ms. Kantor said. "Why don't you go to the cafeteria and carry in the jugs of cider?"

Abby's father reached into his pocket. "I'd like to buy a ticket," he said.

"You're one of our first customers," Ms. Kantor said. "Mason is all set to take your money."

"Step right this way, sir," Mason said smoothly.

In the gym, a crew of kids in costumes was unfolding metal chairs and setting them in rows.

A scattering of people sat near the front. Abby counted them. There were twelve adults and kids.

"Why are there so few people?" Natalie demanded.

Abby jumped. She hadn't realized that Natalie was right behind her.

"Uh, well," Abby began.

Natalie didn't wait for an answer. She hurried away.

Abby took a deep breath and went to get a couple of chairs. She set them at the end of a row. Then she got some more.

Ms. Kantor came into the gym and surveyed the rows of chairs.

"Good job, chair crew!" She glanced at the clock, then at the people trickling into the gym.

She turned on the microphone.

"Good evening," Ms. Kantor greeted the audience. "Popcorn, brownies, and cider are for sale in the cafeteria. The movie will begin a little later than scheduled to give more people a chance to arrive. All profits will be donated to a disaster relief fund."

Mason was standing in front of the ticket table, talking to Bethany and Natalie.

"How many people have come in?" Natalie asked.

"Seventeen?" Mason said. "Maybe eighteen?"

Ms. Kantor hurried toward them. She checked her watch, then glanced at the front doors. The lobby was empty.

"Why isn't anyone here?" she asked. "I don't understand it."

Abby thought of the relief fund. Ms. Kantor's class wouldn't have any money to send to it now. Maybe enough for a couple of boxes of cereal, if they were lucky.

It should have been more.

"I got the posters out too late!" Abby cried. "No one saw them!"

Natalie frowned. Bethany and Mason looked surprised. Ms. Kantor cleared her throat.

"Abby, I wish you had spoken to me sooner," Ms. Kantor began.

"Sorry," Abby said miserably. "I'm really sorry."

The doors flew open. Brianna and Victoria entered the school.

Brianna was dressed as an enchantress in brilliant fire-red satin. She wore red high heels and red lipstick to match. She had a red sparkly crown in her long dark hair and a diamond necklace.

Her new best friend, Victoria, was dressed in a

blue lace T-shirt with a blue leather skirt and chunky shoes.

"You, like, look like a fire engine," she said to her best friend, loud enough for the rest of the class to hear.

"I'm in costume," Brianna announced haughtily.

"You're also late," Ms. Kantor said. "I asked everyone to be here before seven."

"Did you hear the radio announcement?" Brianna asked, putting her hand on her hip. "It said — "

"There wasn't any radio announcement," Abby mumbled. Her face was hot. "I called them too late!"

Brianna cut her off. "You don't have connections. My third cousin's aunt's brother-in-law *owns* the radio station. They've been announcing the Silver Screen Savers movie night every hour for the last three days. Don't you listen to WLXPOP, Tiffany Crystal's favorite station?"

"No," Abby said.

Brianna flipped her long dark hair over her shoulder. "Thanks to me, we'll have a crowd tonight."

"A *crowd*?" Natalie asked, gesturing at the empty lobby.

"Like, where is it?" Victoria said meanly. "I don't see any, like, sixth-grade boys, you know."

"The whole world listens to WLXPOP," Brianna said with a small shrug. "They'll be here. The people will come."

"For once, I hope she's right," Abby whispered to Casey, who had just joined them. "If she is, I'll be the first to yell, 'Yay, Brianna!' "

Ms. Kantor looked at her watch again. "There are no crowds. The movie was supposed to start ten minutes ago, and no one is here."

"The movie is supposed to start at seven-thirty," Brianna said smugly. "The radio announced the wrong time."

"It did??" Ms. Kantor cried.

"The posters and flyers announced seven P.M.," Abby said.

"No one reads those things!" Brianna dismissed her with a wave of the hand.

"Brianna," Ms. Kantor said, frowning. "Why didn't you tell us sooner?"

"Yeah!" Mason echoed. "How were we supposed to know?"

"Like, what's your problem, Tuxedo Man?" Victoria was suddenly on Brianna's side again. "Don't you listen to WLXPOP?"

"No!" Mason retorted.

"I don't listen to it, either," Natalie said.

"Me, neither," Bethany chirped.

"Or me!" Abby said.

"Where do they, like, come from?" Victoria asked her best friend.

Brianna adjusted her crown. "WLXPOP is the best station in town. The crowd will be here."

Ms. Kantor shook her head. "If the crowd doesn't show up *very soon*, I'm starting the movie."

"You'll see," Brianna promised.

The fifth-graders looked at each other. Mason burped. Natalie whispered to Bethany. Casey hummed a tune.

Brianna smiled at her reflection in the glass of the front doors. "Look!" she said, pointing triumphantly.

A group of people was approaching the front door.

Chapter 14

Friday

"A hard beginning makes a good ending."

Days of Winter Calendar

Lots of people are here to see <u>Merlin's Magic School</u>! Mason can't sell tickets fast enough. Casey, Natalie, and Bethany are helping him. Almost every seat is filled!!!

Our hard beginning <u>didn't</u> make this good ending! Brianna made it.

Thanks to her, we will meet our expenses and have a large donation for the relief fund.

Thanks to her, our movie night is a success!

Thanks to her, I'm off the hook.

Sometimes Brianna really _is_ the best!

In recognition of her service to Ms. Kantor's fifth-grade class and to me, <u>The Hayes Book of World Records</u> will award Brianna a free one-day brag pass. She is entitled to unlimited bragging for twenty-four hours. No one will be allowed to complain!

Okay, I <u>promised</u> I'd do it:

Yay, Brianna. Yay, Brianna! <u>YAY, BRI-ANNA!</u>

P.S. I have only one problem left.
Who am I going to sit with?

Natalie: Tells me what to do all the time now. Do I want to be lectured on my mistakes?
Sarah: Just don't like her very much.
Bethany: Sitting with Natalie and Sarah.
Casey: I'd like to sit with him, but if I do, my friends will tease me, and Brianna and Victoria will call us lovebirds.

Mason: No, I don't think I want to sit with the Big Burper.
Jessica: In Oregon and mad at me.

I guess I'll sit by myself.

Who cares??? Our movie night is a success!!!! Hooray!!!!

Abby stood at the bathroom sink, washing her hands. They were sticky from the jelly donuts she had eaten.

The movie was over. Now everyone was in the cafeteria feasting on Toad's Blood, Merlin's Brew, Gobbles, and Dragon Rings.

Abby dried her hands and checked her costume in the mirror. Her silver-foil pen nib was off to the side of her head. She adjusted it and brushed donut crumbs from the front of her robe.

For what seemed like the thousandth time that evening, she breathed a sigh of relief.

"This thing is *so* hot!" Bethany cried, coming into the bathroom. She pulled off her costume's hamster head. "You're smiling, Abby."

"Our Silver Screen Savers movie night was a success!" Abby explained.

Bethany splashed water on her flushed face. "Of course it was. Why wouldn't it be?"

"*Me*," Abby said. "Didn't you hear? I got the posters up late!" She sighed. "I wish no one knew. Especially Natalie."

"Why?" Bethany asked. "I thought you were best friends."

Abby shrugged.

"It's just a mistake," Bethany said.

"I've made a *lot* of them," Abby said. "Especially since Jessica left. I haven't been myself in a while."

"Who's that?" Bethany teased.

She gave Abby a quick hug. "Natalie will understand."

"Maybe," Abby said. She hoped Bethany was right. "Too bad Elaine won't," she added.

"Elaine?" Bethany wiped her face with a paper towel.

"Geoffrey's mother." Abby lowered her voice. "I got fired from my baby-sitting job. All I did was forget one time."

"That's too bad," Bethany said sympathetically.

"I wish she had given me another chance,"

Abby said. "Or maybe not. Geoffrey is a handful."

Bethany giggled. "I heard about the maple syrup in Jessica's hair."

"He's a terror with chocolate pudding, too."

Bethany lowered the hamster head back onto her head. "How does Jessica do it?"

"She had special Geoffrey-taming tricks." Abby sighed. "And she never forgets anything."

Bethany waved to Abby. "See you at the refreshment stand?"

Abby bent down to tie her sneaker. A toilet flushed, and one of the stall doors swung open.

A woman came out and glanced at Abby. She went to the sink and turned on the water.

Abby stood up. She brushed off her robe one last time. Her eyes met the eyes of the woman in the mirror. It was Elaine.

"Uh . . ." she stammered. "Uh . . ."

Elaine's lips tightened. She turned off the water, dried her hands with a paper towel, and hurried away without a word.

Her face burning, Abby stumbled out of the bathroom.

Had Elaine heard *every* word she said?

In the cafeteria, a group of fifth-graders gathered to watch Mason pop donuts in his mouth, one after another.

"Six, seven, eight," the kids chanted.

"How many donuts can Mason eat?" Natalie cried.

"Like, millions," Victoria said.

"Urp," Mason said.

"Join us!" Casey called.

Abby gazed miserably around her. The last thing she wanted was to watch a donut-eating contest. Why hadn't she talked about hamsters, Bethany's favorite subject?

Her father tapped her on the shoulder. "It's time to leave," he said.

"Good," Abby said.

"The movie was great!" Alex cried. He had come with his friend Peter. "Did you like it, Abby?"

"Sure." She pulled her coat over her costume and followed her father, her brother, and his friend out to the parking lot.

Paul Hayes unlocked the van. "Everyone in!" he ordered.

Alex and Peter tumbled into the backseat.

Her father put his hand on Abby's shoulder. "You should be proud of yourself, honey," he said. "It was a terrific fund-raiser!"

"Thanks," Abby mumbled.

Her father brushed a light dusting of snow from the windshield.

Abby glanced at her classmates returning to their cars. Brianna and Victoria were arguing loudly as Brianna's mother honked the horn to get their attention.

"Just a minute, Dad," Abby said suddenly. "I'll be right back."

She dashed across the lot and came to a halt, breathless, in front of Elaine and Geoffrey.

Chapter 15

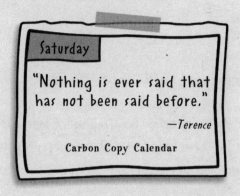

Saturday

"Nothing is ever said that has not been said before."

—Terence

Carbon Copy Calendar

<u>What I said to Elaine</u>
1. "Um, uh . . ."
2. "Uh, I, uh . . ."
3. "I, uh, well . . ."
4. "Oh, uh, um . . ."

Has anyone said this before? I hope so. I'd hate to be the first person who stuttered and stammered this way.

<u>What I said to Elaine next</u>
1. "I, uh, um . . . I'm . . ."
2. "I'm, uh, ssss – "

3. "What I, um . . . I mean . . .
uh . . ."
4. "Well . . . oh . . . uh . . . uh . . ."

Has someone said that, too?

Elaine didn't say anything. She just
waited. If she had said something, it might
have been easier. It also might have been
harder.

Finally I took a breath. "I - I'm sorry I
forgot about baby-sitting Geoffrey."

Elaine nodded.

"Um . . . I hope I never do it again."

"I hope not," Elaine said. She didn't
look too friendly. "If it hadn't been for
your sister, I would have lost a morning's
work."

"Sorry!" I said.

Geoffrey made a face at me.

"Jessica never forgot," Elaine continued.
"I thought you'd be reliable."

"It was just once," I muttered miserably.

"Once too many," Elaine said.

"Sorry," I said again.

Elaine didn't reply.

"Well, see you around," I said.

I ran back to the car.

My father was sitting behind the wheel. As I slid into the front seat, he patted my arm.

"That took courage," he said.

"Really?"

"Yes!" my father said.

"It didn't go very well," I mumbled.

"You apologized, didn't you?" he asked.

"Yes, but — "

"She was still angry?"

I nodded.

"Then it took even more courage to apologize," my father said.

"Well . . ."

"I'm proud of you." My father turned the key in the ignition and backed slowly out of the parking space.

"Really?" I didn't believe him.

"You faced up to a mistake. You didn't run away from what you had done."

I took a deep breath. "I was trying to do something right for a change."

My father nodded. "You won't ever forget a baby-sitting date again," he promised.

"No!" I cried. "I'll tie a hundred pieces of string around my fingers, write the times on every calendar in my room, put signs on the bathroom mirror and the front and back doors . . . "

Alex leaned forward. "I'll put a reminder in the computer for you, Abby," he offered.

"Okay," I said. "It's a deal."

Bethany just called. We made $418.50 for the relief fund!

Hooray! Hooray! Hooray!

Ms. Kantor said to Natalie and Bethany and Mason that she was very proud of the entire class. She called the newspaper to tell them what we had done. A photographer will come to our class on Monday. We are going to have our pictures in the paper.

Speaking of relief . . .

I am more relieved than anyone in the

fifth grade!!! My bad luck has finally broken!!

PHEW!!!! Stretch arms and touch toes. Hop around purple room. Pick up phone and call Jessica in Oregon. Has my bad luck broken there, too?

She hasn't written me in more than a week. I <u>HAVE</u> to know if we're still friends.

<u>Notes after a Phone Conversation</u>
1. What the girl who answered the phone called her: "Jessy."
2. Who Jessica thought I was: Someone named Madison.
3. When Jessica got my e-mail: More than a week ago.
4. Why she didn't write back: She forgot. (<u>Ha!</u> So I'm NOT the only one!!!)
5. What she talked about: Dances, boys, lip gloss, new clothes.
6. What she didn't talk about: Our friends, science, drawing, Ms. Kantor's class, movie night.

glossy gloss
* * *

7. What I said: Almost nothing.

8. How the conversation ended: Danielle called for Jessy to help her pick the right necklace for the dance tonight.

The Good News

Jessica isn't mad at me anymore.

The Bad News

Who is Jessy?

The Old News

I miss Jessica.

The New News

Jessy doesn't miss me.

The Worst News

Jessy and I don't have much in common. We might not even like each other anymore. This is even more horrible than Jessica being mad at me!

What to Do

1. Cry.
2. Write in journal.
3. Look at face in mirror.
4. Comb hair. Wipe eyes. Stick out tongue.
5. Start to cry again.

INTERRUPTION! Alex just knocked on the door. Casey is here to see me.

What to Do, Part Two

1. Wipe eyes again. Blow nose. Make face at self in mirror.
2. Put on sunglasses to hide red eyes.
3. Go downstairs. Say hi to Casey.
4. Say yes when Casey asks if I want to ride my bike with him this afternoon.

Go outside. See bright sunshine. Take deep breath. Climb on bike. Ride to park and race Casey around the fountain. Win. Laugh. Race again.

MORE SERIES YOU'LL FALL IN LOVE WITH

Heartland™

Nestled in the foothills of Virginia, there's a place where horses come when they are hurt. Amy, Ty, and everyone at Heartland work together to heal the horses—and form lasting bonds that will touch your heart.

The AMAZING DAYS of ABBY HAYES™

In a family of superstars, it's hard to stand out. But Abby is about to surprise her friends, her family, and most of all, herself!

Jody is about to begin a dream vacation on the wide open sea, traveling to new places and helping her parents with their dolphin research. You can tag along with

Dolphin Diaries™

**Learn more at
www.scholastic.com/books**

Available Wherever Books Are Sold.